SUPERWORM

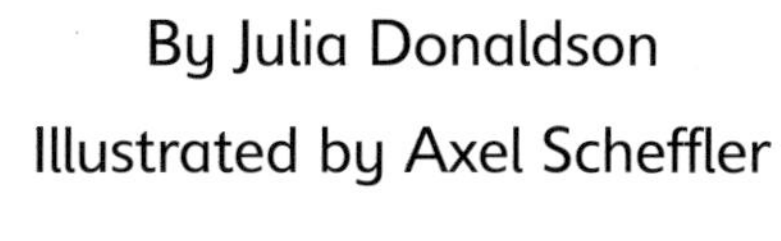

By Julia Donaldson

Illustrated by Axel Scheffler

Superworm is super-long.

Superworm is super-strong.

Watch him wiggle! See him squirm!

Hip, hip, hooray for SUPERWORM!

Help! Disaster! Baby toad
Has hopped on to a major road.

"Quick! Whatever can we do?"

Look – a SUPERWORM lasso!

The bees are feeling bored today.

They need a nice new game to play.

Cheer up, bees! No need to mope . . .

It's SUPERWORM, the skipping-rope!

Beetle's fallen in the well!

Is she drowning? Who can tell?

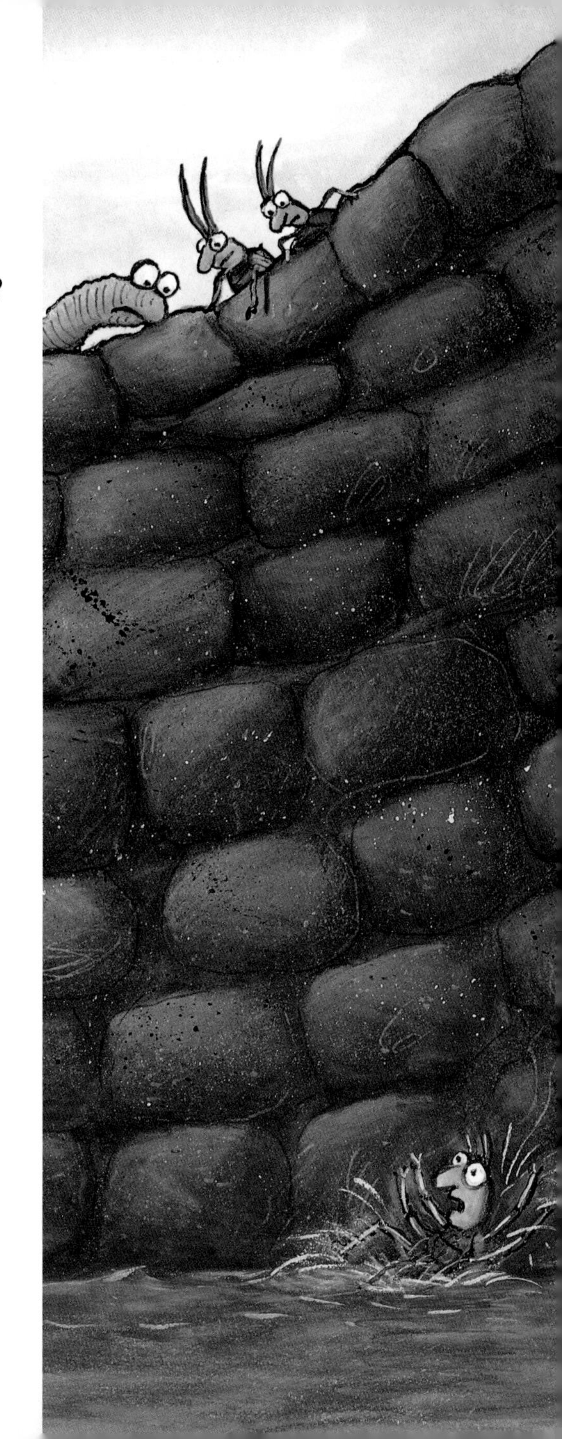

Not to panic – all is fine . . .

It's SUPERWORM, the fishing-line!

Then toads and beetles, bees and bugs,
Brother snails and sister slugs,
Uncle ant and earwig aunt
Clap and cheer and chant this chant:

"Superworm is super-long.
Superworm is super-strong.
Watch him wiggle! See him squirm!
Hip, hip, hooray for SUPERWORM!"

The chant is carried on the air
To Wizard Lizard in his lair.
He mutters in his servant's ear,
"Find that worm and bring him here."

The servant crow is black and grim.
Everyone is scared of him.
They all let out a fearful shriek
To see their hero in his beak.

The wizard waves his magic flower.
"Now, Superworm, you're in my power
And you must tunnel, writhe and coil,
To find me treasure in the soil."

Superworm is very cross
To have a lizard as his boss,
But when he tries to slink away
The wizard's magic makes him stay.

For days he tunnels, twists and winds,
But all the treasure that he finds
Is two small buttons, half a cork,
A toffee and a plastic fork.

The lizard flicks an angry tail.
"Have one last try, and if you fail
To find that treasure down below,
I'll feed you to my hungry crow."

CHATE
MIS EN B

The crow is flapping through the night.
Everyone looks up in fright.
They see him perch upon an oak
And listen to his dreadful croak:

"Superworm is good to eat!
Superworm's a special treat!
He'll be juicy, fat and firm.
Hip, hip, hooray for SUPERWORM!"

"Action! Quickly! At the double!
Superworm's in frightful trouble!
We must help him if we can.
We must hatch a cunning plan!"

The garden creatures leave their home,
Carrying a honeycomb.

They jump and fly and crawl and creep . . .

. . . and find the lizard fast asleep.

They chew the petals off his flower
To rob him of his magic power.

The caterpillars fetch some leaves,

While busily the spider weaves.

The web is strong. The web is tough.

The web is plenty big enough.

The wizard wakes. "This isn't funny!

I'm wrapped in leaves and stuck with honey!"

Then up the bees and beetles fly
And lift the web into the sky.

"This is the place!" and . . .

BANG! CRASH! THUMP!

The wizard's in the rubbish dump!

And now, from somewhere underground
There comes a distant rumbling sound.
The earth begins to heave, and then . . .

SUPERWORM is back again!

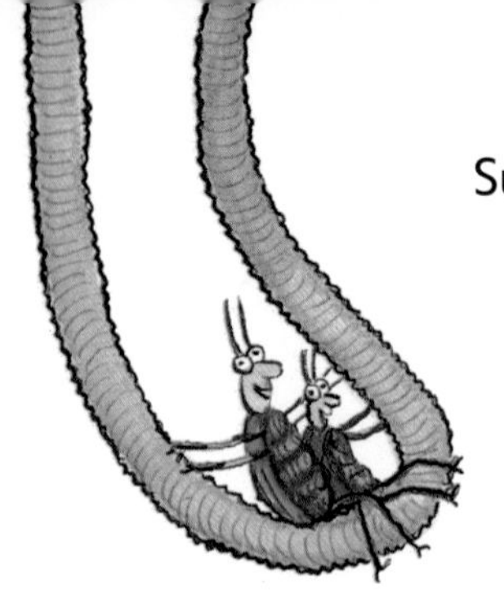

Superworm, the swing!

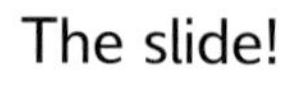

The slide!

The hula-hoop!

The fairground ride!

Superworm, the belt!

The hat!

The crane!

The train!

The acrobat!

Then toads and beetles, bees and bugs,
Brother snails and sister slugs,
Uncle ant and earwig aunt
Clap and cheer and chant this chant:

"Superworm is super-long.
Superworm is super-strong.
Watch him wiggle! See him squirm!
Hip, hip, hooray for SUPERWORM!"

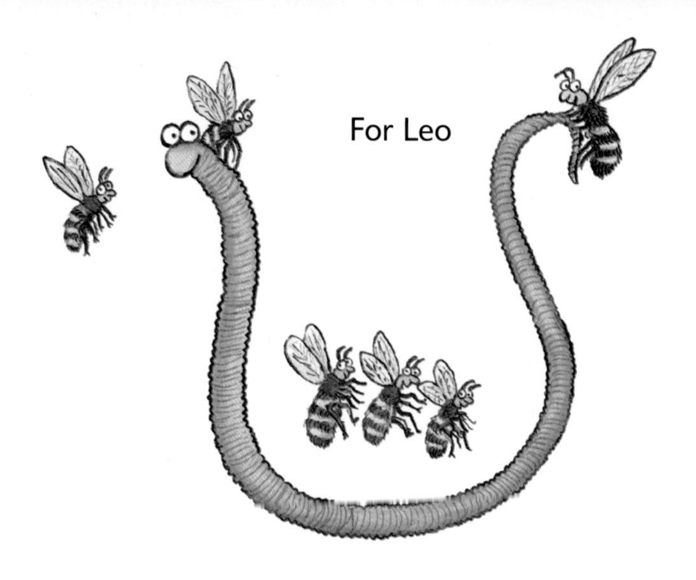

For Leo

First published in the UK in 2012 by
Alison Green Books
An imprint of Scholastic Children's Books
Euston House, 24 Eversholt Street
London NW1 1DB, UK
A division of Scholastic Ltd
www.scholastic.co.uk
London – New York – Toronto – Sydney – Auckland
Mexico City – New Delhi – Hong Kong
This Early Reader edition first published in 2016

ISBN: 978 1 407166 08 7

Printed in Malaysia.

1 3 5 7 9 10 8 6 4 2